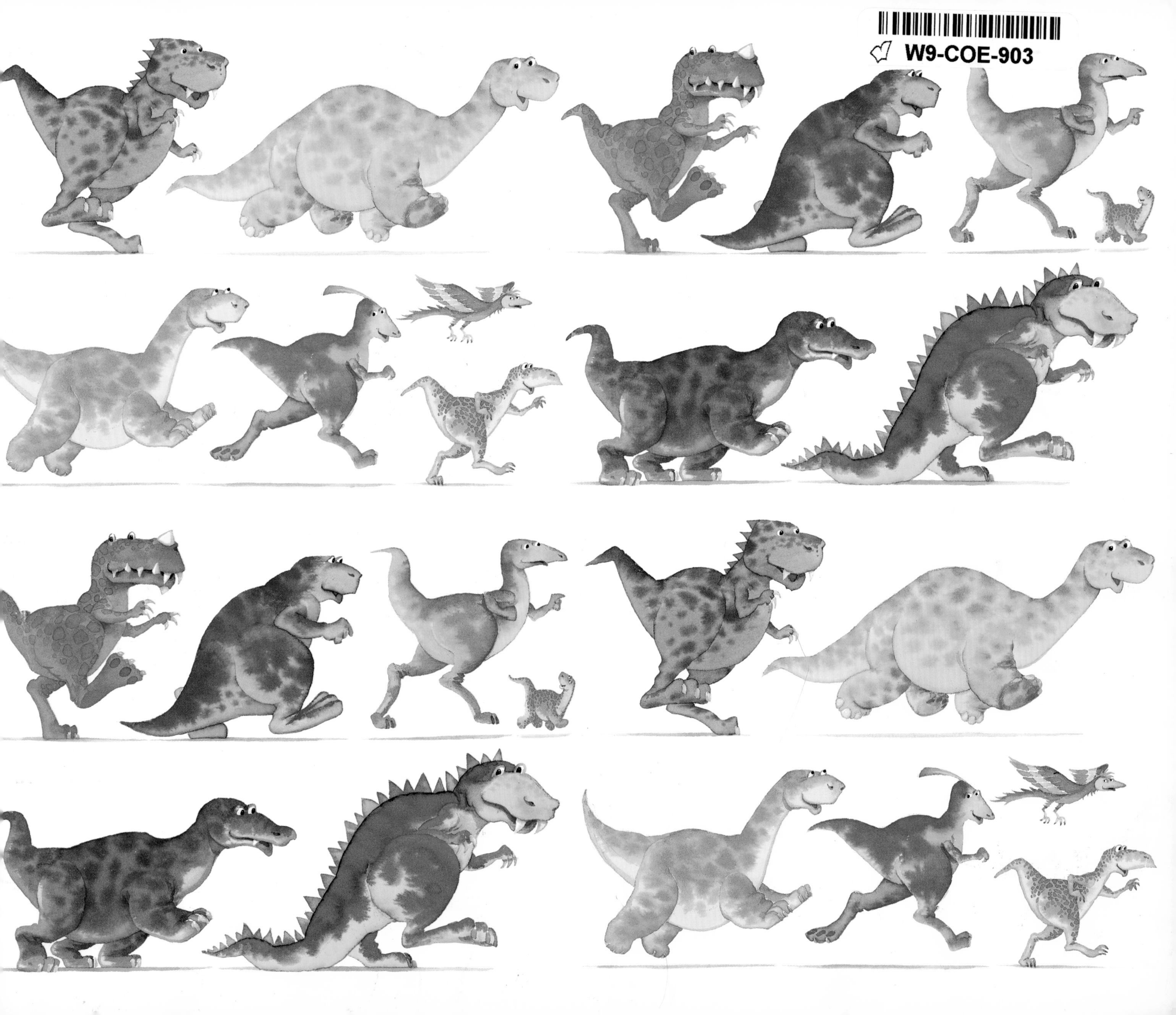

**Library of Congress Cataloging-in-Publication Data**

Stickland, Paul.
Dinosaur roar!/by Paul and Henrietta Stickland.—1st American ed. p. cm.
"Originally published in Great Britain, 1994,
by Ragged Bears Limited, Hampshire, England"—T.p. verso.
Summary: Illustrations and rhyming text present all kinds of
dinosaurs, including ones that are sweet, grumpy, spiky, or lumpy.
ISBN 0-525-45276-1
[1. Dinosaurs—Fiction. 2. Stories in rhyme.]
I. Stickland, Henrietta. II. Title.
PZ8.3.S854Di 1994 [E]—dc20 93-43959 CIP AC

First published in the United States 1994
by Dutton Children's Books,
a member of Penguin Putnam Inc.
375 Hudson Street, New York, New York 10014

Typography by Amy Berniker
Printed in Hong Kong
First American Edition
9 10 8

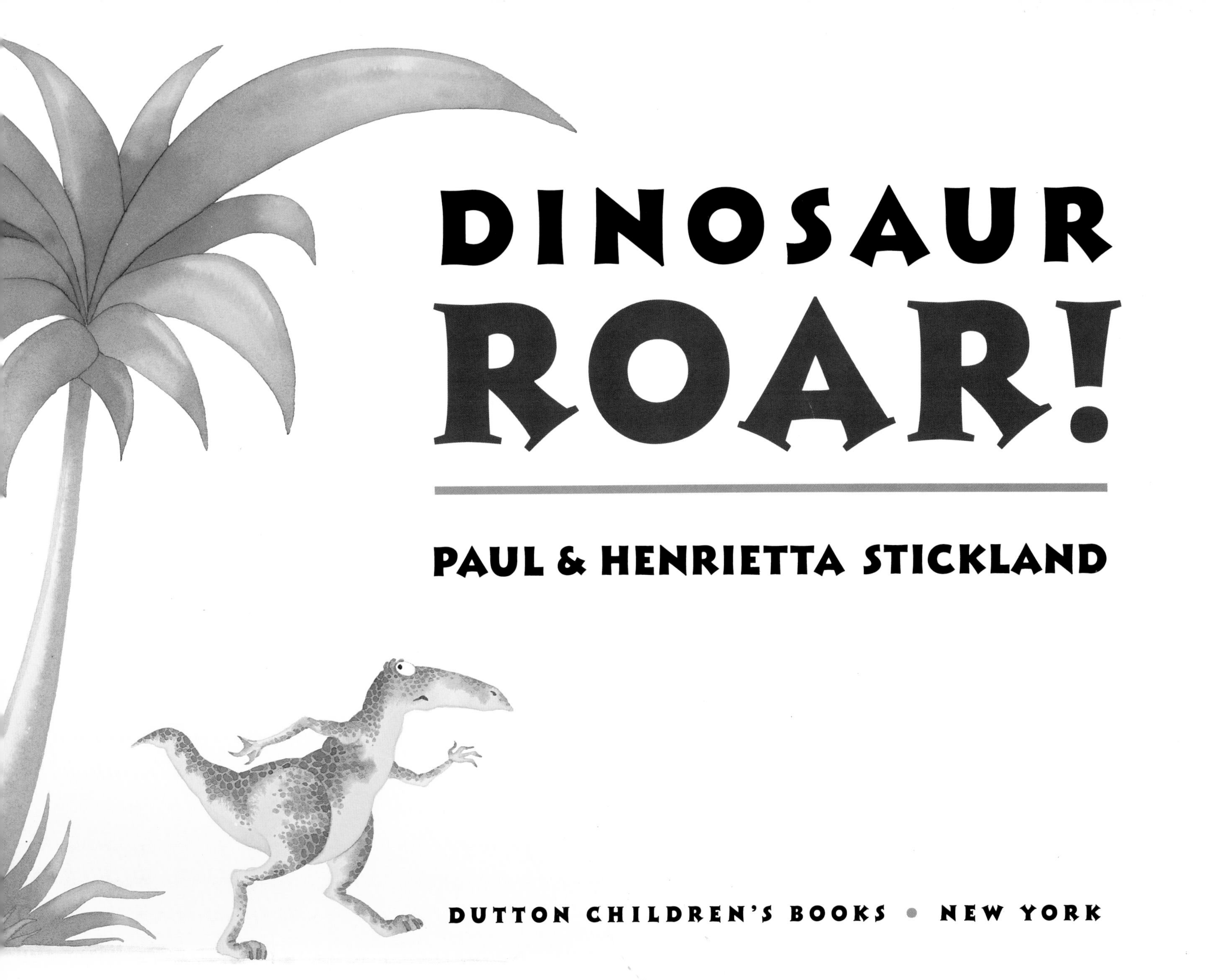

# DINOSAUR ROAR!

PAUL & HENRIETTA STICKLAND

DUTTON CHILDREN'S BOOKS • NEW YORK

Dinosaur roar,

dinosaur squeak,

dinosaur fierce,

dinosaur meek,

dinosaur fast,

dinosaur slow,

dinosaur above

and dinosaur below.

Dinosaur weak,

dinosaur strong,

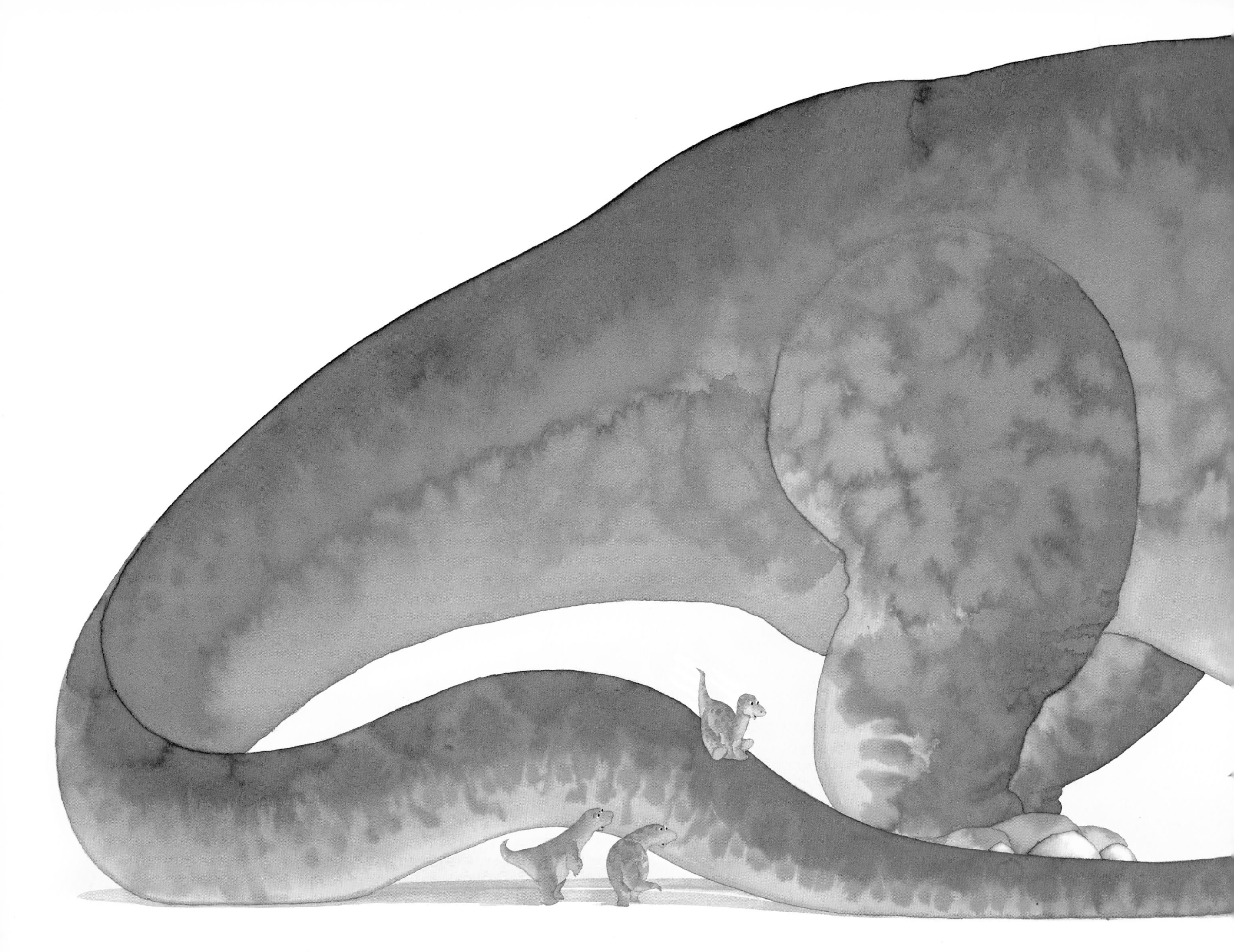

dinosaur short

or very, very long.

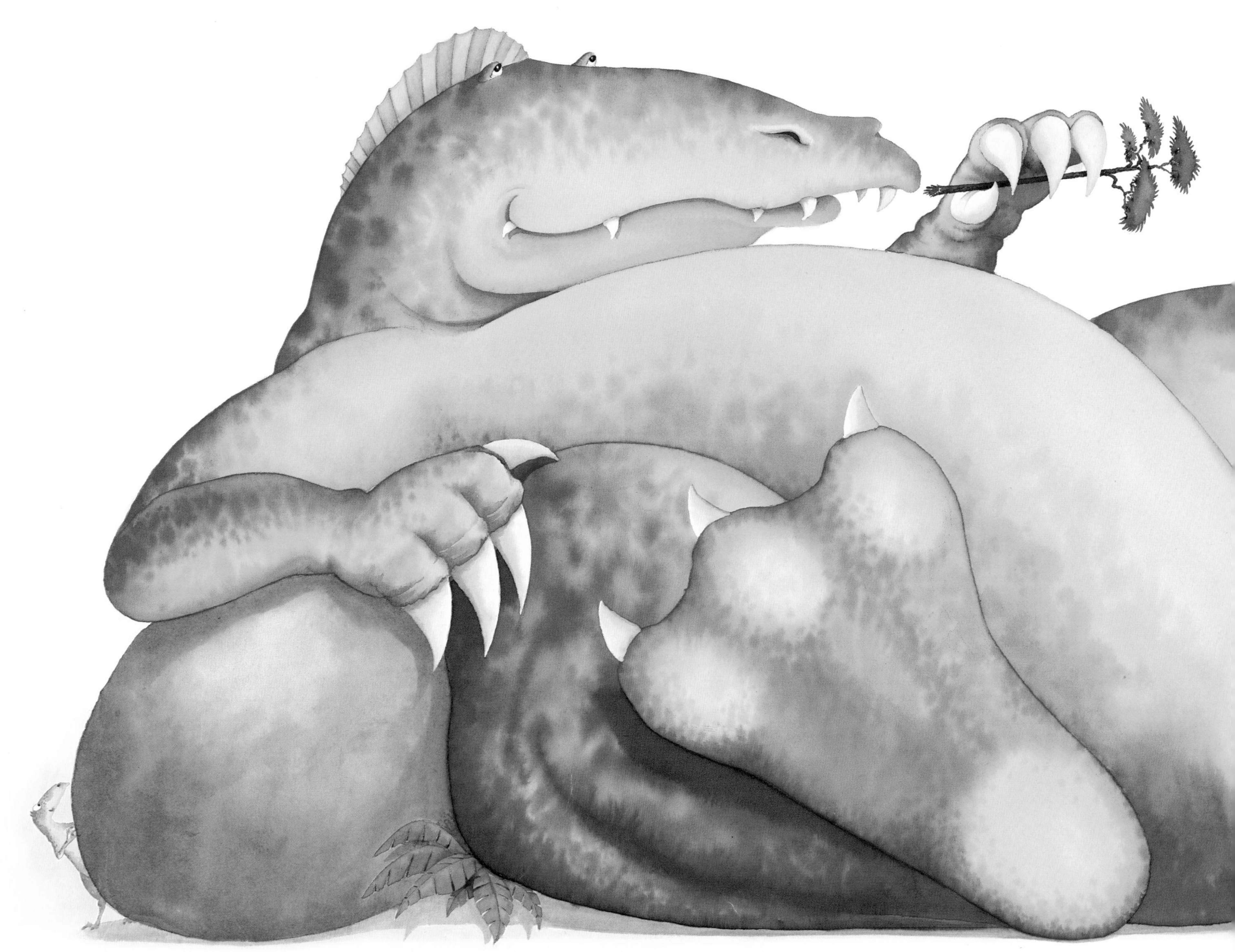

Dinosaur fat,

dinosaur tiny,

dinosaur clean

and dinosaur slimy.

Dinosaur sweet,

dinosaur grumpy,

dinosaur spiky

and dinosaur lumpy.

# All sorts of dinosaurs

eating their lunch,

gobble, gobble, nibble, nibble,

munch, munch, scrunch!